JE
BRI

Brimner, Lar
Dane.
Dinosaurs d

DINOSAURS DANCE

By Larry Dane Brimner

Illustrated by Patrick Girouard

Children's Press®
A Division of Grolier Publishing
New York • London • Hong Kong • Sydney
Danbury, Connecticut

For Jacob Keeser
–L. D. B.

For my friends at the White Oak School
–P. G.

Reading Consultant
Linda Cornwell
Learning Resource Consultant
Indiana Department of Education

Visit Children's Press® on the Internet at:
http://publishing.grolier.com

Library of Congress Cataloging-in-Publication Data
Brimner, Larry Dane.
Dinosaurs dance / by Larry Dane Brimner ; illustrated by Patrick Girouard.
p. cm. — (A rookie reader)
Summary: Though other animals may twirl and prance, there is nothing like a dinosaur dance.
ISBN 0-516-20752-0 (lib. bdg.)   0-516-26358-7 (pbk.)
[1. Dinosaurs—Fiction. 2. Dance—Fiction. 3. Stories in rhyme.] I. Girouard, Patrick, ill. II. Title. III.
Series.
PZ8.3.B77145Di 1998
[E] —dc21
97-18798
CIP
AC

Dinosaurs roar.

Dinosaurs rock.

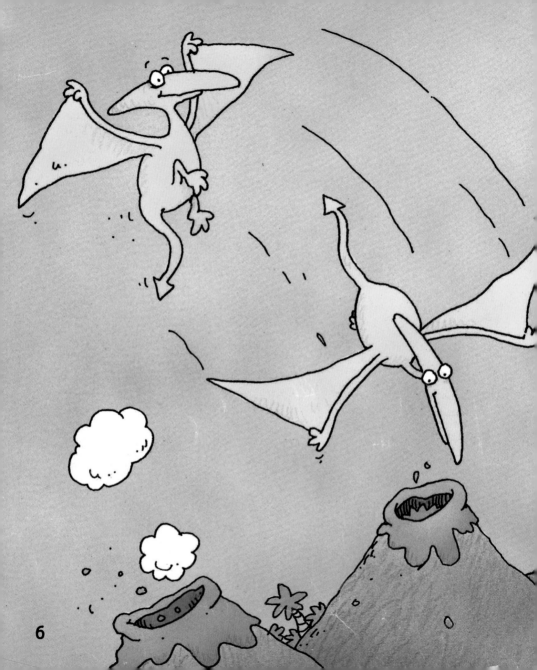

6

Dinosaurs dip.

Dinosaurs . . . slip!

Dinosaurs sway.

Dinosaurs step.

Dinosaurs hop.

Dinosaurs . . . flop!

Dinosaurs twirl.

Dinosaurs twist.

Dinosaurs shuffle.

Dinosaurs . . . ruffle!

24

Dinosaurs clap.
Dinosaurs clog.

26

Dinosaurs prance.

Dinosaurs . . . DANCE!

About the Author

Larry Dane Brimner writes on a wide range of topics, from picture book and middle-grade fiction to young adult nonfiction. His previous Rookie Readers are *Brave Mary, Firehouse Sal, How Many Ants?* and *Lightning Liz.* Mr. Brimner is also the author of *E-mail* and *The World Wide Web* for Children's Press and the award-winning *Merry Christmas, Old Armadillo* (Boyds Mills Press). He lives in the southwest region of the United States.

About the Illustrator

Patrick Girouard was born small but grew and grew and then one day stopped growing. He went to regular school first and art school next. He has two beautiful sons called Marc and Max. They all live in Indiana. He loves a red-haired lady, dogs, bagels, coffee, making pictures, naps, and many other things too numerous to mention.